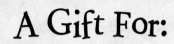

A Gift For:

Ava and Olivia

From:

Your Elf ♡

Editor: Jared Smith
Art Director: Chris Opheim
Designer: Bryan Ring
Production Designer: Bryan Ring

ISBN: 978-1-59530-553-4
LPR2342

Printed and bound in China
JUL12

There's Snow Stopping Us Now!

Written by Cheryl Hawkinson

Illustrated by Mike Esberg

'Twas the day of the annual Mount Icy Run

and the whole town of Snowbelt was ready for fun.

Snow folks had gathered from far and from near

for the iciest race in the north hemisphere.

Then, all of a sudden, from up in the sky,
a big box came falling. What was it, and why?

When all of the snow folks crept closer to look,
a voice squeaked out "Help!" and the box rocked and shook.

And out popped a penguin with a mischievous smile,

who flashed them a note in a confident style:

The people of Snowbelt were totally stunned.
"Why did you come here? Where are you from?"

"Are you planning to race? But your skis are so tall!
Are you sure that they'll work? You're so small, after all!

Perry replied, "I'm from the South Pole,

and racing Mount Icy's my big lifetime goal."

"The skis are my grandpa's. They're sweet and they're fast.

They're made out of candy, but they're sure built to last."

"Kid, you've got spunk," said a snow kid named Squee.
"I'll help you get started—just stick close to me."

Then Perry and Squee, and his friends Slick and Stace,
followed the crowds to the site of the race.

They jumped on the ski lift to ride up Mount Icy.

"Hang on, little Perry," said Squee. "This gets dicey."

They rose higher and higher. The wind snapped and twirled.

"Here we go!" cried out Perry, "to the top of the world!"

But once they got up there and Perry looked down,
he started to shiver and quiver and frown.

He thought to himself, "How can steep be so deep?
I don't think I'm ready to make such a leap."

But he just went along with the rest of the throng.
Then the starting bell rang—and something was wrong!

"Oh, no!" shouted Squee. "My Snowfloogle's broken!
My steering is shot and my snack-rack is smokin'!"

Then Perry piped up, "Use my candy cane skis!
I don't mind not racing. Just go ahead, please!"

"Really?" said Squee. "That would be super great.
I'll do you proud, Perry. Just wait at the gate."

Squee put on his skis and tore off down the slope,

with his mind set on winning and his heart full of hope.

But when Perry peered over, he saw that poor Squee

had tangled and mangled his skis in a tree!

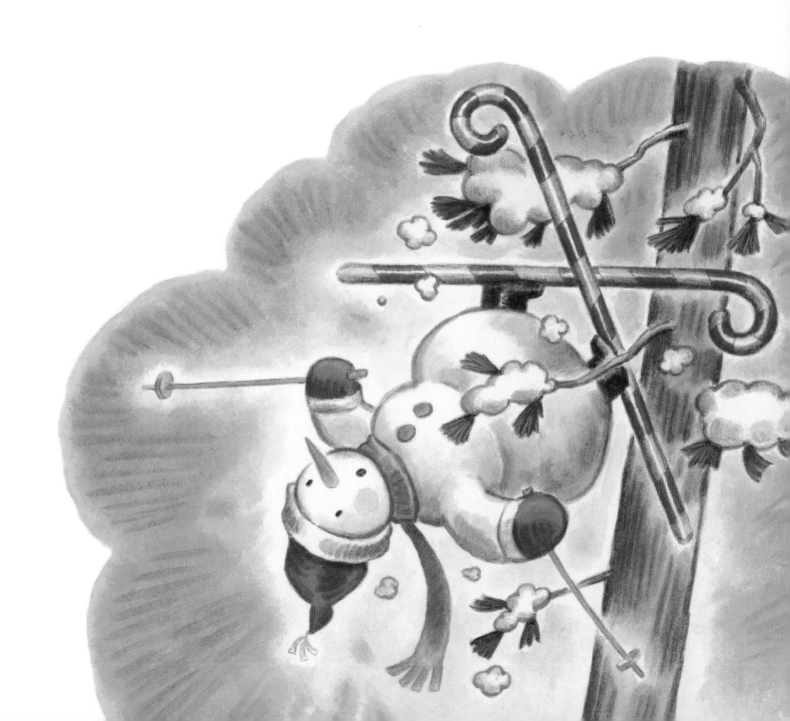

Forgetting his fear, Perry took off to help,
sliding down on his belly with a very loud yelp!

He swooped and he swerved with incredible speed,
landing right at the spot where poor Squee had been treed.

Once Perry freed Squee and they shook off some snow,

they looked at each other and said, "Hey, let's go!"

They raced down together, Perry and Squee,

flying fast past the finish with a whoop and a whee.

"We did it!" said Perry. "My friend and I here!
My big dream came true and I conquered my fear!"

"You did it!" said Squee. "What a guy! What a friend!
That sure was fun, Perry. Let's do it again!"

If this snowy adventure warmed your heart,
or if perhaps you just liked the art,
we would love to hear from you.

PLEASE SEND YOUR COMMENTS TO:
Hallmark Book Feedback
P.O. Box 419034
Mail Drop 215
Kansas City, Missouri 64141

OR E-MAIL US AT:
booknotes@hallmark.com